Stupid Cupid

Holiday Hearts Book 4

By Pixie Chica

Thank You!

Thank you for your purchase Stupid Cupid. I hope you enjoy the story and will consider leaving a review or telling a friend about the book. I love hearing from readers! To keep in touch and follow my news, please visit me at: facebook.com/pixiechicaauthor

Stupid Cupid

by
Pixie Chica

Romeo Cupid Jr.

When my mother declares war on my single-hood, I know it's
time I find a decoy. At 35, I'm the oldest bachelor in the cupid
clan so my meddling mother has concocted a plan to get me
engaged by my sister's wedding. Acting on desperation, I
accept a date-for-hire with a woman named Chels.

It was supposed to be a temporary fix, but once my eyes land
on her, there's no way I'll let her go – Even if she thinks I'm
just a Stupid Cupid.

Looks like I'll be granting my mom's wish after all.

Chelsea "Chels" McQueen

Spinster, cat lady, freak…Yeah I knew the names everyone
called me. That's why I needed to get out of the North Pole,
and quick. Short on cash, and out of options, I accept the job of
girlfriend for a week. How bad could it be for a thousand
bucks? I was expecting an awkward and shy man who was
being tormented about being single.

What I didn't bargain for was the handsome giant I get
instead. He may think he can be boss me like the Neanderthal
he is, but I'll show him.

Just as soon as I stop getting lost in those troubled emerald
eyes.

This Valentine's Day, the reluctant Cupid has met his match.
He'll have to pull out all the stops, and then some.

Dedication

To Heather B. who shot her arrow and claimed Romeo before anyone else.

Note to Reader

In Undercover Santa there was a brief mention of Romeo in the epilogue, but as his story unfolded, I had to change it, otherwise, Stupid Cupid would not be what it is now. The mention of Romeo and Chels in His Christmas Gift has not changed.

Chapter One

~ Romeo Cupid Jr. ~

Ten years ago...

As I was meeting a potential client that would fund my dream of opening a tattoo shop, my mother called screaming about an emergency. Needless to say, the man was not impressed and an email saying he was no longer interested has just hit my phone. It's awful to even think it, but something better seriously be wrong as my one chance to leave the Cupid curse behind, finally prove I'm more than simply a glorified matchmaker, is now gone.

Exiting the small charter plane that'd been waiting for me, I take a deep breath at the realization I'm in Heartland again, aka home to all the Cupids. I'd graduated college six months ago, and shortly after that had told my mother I wasn't coming back. Of course, that was not only unheard of but also a big no-no. In this family, being Cupid is not only what you do, but also who you are, and what you were remembered for when you died.

Every single minute of my life had involved teaching me how to recognize the signs, to arrow someone without getting caught. It's a little-known fact, but all those magical creatures everyone assumes aren't real, do exist. We actually live in adjoining cities. To the right of my hometown is the North Pole where my aunt lives with the Clauses. The Cupids are in the middle and the Lanterns are to the left in Hollow's Cove. We tended to stay in our own area, though we could and sometimes did move freely between the lands.

There are many Cupids, however, I'm descended from the original, and my mother, who had been somewhat obsessed with Romeo himself, eventually married him. After that, she became the ultimate matriarch, intent on her mission of marrying me off since the day I turned eighteen. Thankfully, she now focused on the twins since they've hit twenty, as the majority of Cupids were already married by twenty-one, a milestone I've passed.

Standing on the other side of the small shop, that doubles as the airport, is Luca. He's a good friend, but he's also dating one of my twin sisters, Milena, so I have to give him a hard time. His own twin, Stefano, has been spending a lot of time with my other sister, Passion. Not only am I the lone boy amongst my parents five children, I'm also the oldest which makes me super protective. That being said, there's no one else I'd rather have Milena with. It's his brother I'm not sure of as he's too quiet, the complete opposite of the over-the-top Passion.

"Welcome home," Luca greets me with a bro hug. "I'm here to take you to your mom's."

I follow him to his car, double-checking and ribbing him at the same time with, "So, in the couple months I've been gone, you haven't fucked up with my sister, right? I will Arrow her to another guy if you do." Luca and his family settled here a couple of years ago when his father became city manager. As he still doesn't quite grasp how everything works, I enjoy messing with his ass whenever possible.

"Nice try. Milena, who I'm asking to marry me tonight, told me Cupids aren't allowed to do that to themselves or their family. Oh," he adds, as if I'm not in enough shock, states, "and Stefano is proposing to Passion."

"What the fuck, man? How the hell can you just blurt that out?" I want to know, serious as fuck. I don't want to meddle in my sisters' lives, but this is too quick, and screams of my mother's doing.

"Dude, I know you're going to say we're too young, but I fucking love her more than anyone else ever will and I'll do everything in my power to make her happy. I'm glad your mom suggested it." He runs a hand through his hair, obviously uncomfortable discussing this, and informs me, "You're my friend and I'd hoped you'd be excited for us, but Stefano and I already talked about this.

We're marrying them with or without your blessing."

I'm silent for a few minutes, his determination as clear as the anger rising within him, I decide to cut the guy some slack and chuckle. "Jeez, you'd think you were born into the damn family the way you went all gung-ho for your woman. Remember this, though. Either of you step out on them, I will make you regret it."

"I would never. She's the most gorgeous woman in the world and I've been counting the days until she's officially mine. Milena will be my first, and I'll be hers."

"Woahhhhh! No, just no. That's fucking sweet and all, but no! Do not talk about you and my sister doing anything other than going on picnics and shit." I shake my head and shudder at the mere mention of their love life while getting in the car.

Once I'm inside and he takes off, it hits me. There was no fucking emergency, just the impromptu engagement. And I fell for it. When Luca confirms it, I have an almost uncontrollable urge to punch something. She ruined my dream due to her need to follow traditions, meaning all the male relatives have to be in attendance when a woman gets engaged, and the reverse goes for a man getting engaged. I've always hated these rituals, and I'll be reiterating that when I see her.

But once more, what I want has to wait because a party is in full swing and mom immediately rushes to take my arm and lead me to the middle of the floor toward a poor woman that appears as reluctant to be there as I am.

"Romeo, sweetie, I know I was all kinds of secretive, but I found your one! You're twenty-five now and your younger sisters can't get married before you, so I fixed it. This is Maisy Holland; her dad works with yours. Isn't that right, babe?"

"Yup," is all my dad says before taking a swig of his beer. The man will never deny her anything as he's fucking crazy over her, but this is too far.

"Mom, stop it. I can't believe you did this shit to me! I had a shot at the shop, and you knew it. You knew how important today was to my future. Why would you do this to me? I'm gone," I unload my frustration as I head the other way.

"You were being foolish. Once a Cupid, always a Cupid, you know that. You want to be disowned and put on the banned list over some stupid pipe dream? You belong here with your family." She touches my arm, but I move it out of her reach, causing the room to gasp in horror.

"Being born to make others fall in love, hoping to God you didn't pick the wrong one by trusting instincts that aren't one hundred percent foolproof, is stupid. You want me here, running this damn ideal that we're all meant to shoot fucking arrows? Fine. But heed this, you can't make me fall in love no matter how hard you try." And then I storm off, not caring if I ruined my sisters' party.

"Romeo Cupid! You will not disrespect your mother," my dad snaps at me. However, I'm too far gone to stop. I need fresh air and time to accept what I never wanted to be a part of. My fate is sealed, so what's the point of trying when she'd continually find a way to stop me at every turn? Jumping on my motorcycle that I'd left there last time I was at my parent's house, I go for a ride, taking the path that borders the North Pole. My only goal right now is to stop at my favorite place to relax, which means I pay no attention to the shadow, as if someone else had the same idea I did. Solace. Wonder what they're trying to outrun?

Chapter Two

~ Chelsea "Chels" McQueen ~

Finally! I can leave and find my own path in life. My bags are packed, and my bank account is, too, thanks to my inheritance from Aunt Lydia. I'm so tired of hearing my parents argue about everything, including how much they hate each other, and now I no longer have to. I turned eighteen yesterday and have already graduated, so I'm using my one-way ticket to get out of the North Pole. Yup, you heard right.

My family is among the select few that work for good ole' St. Nick. Gregory Claus is a nice person, as is his wife, Genevieve. Their daughter, Brandie, is one of my friends. While others view the Clauses as the bosses, I see them as the perfect example of what parents should be. Loving, caring, and worthy of the title. They didn't hesitate to let me know I was welcome to come back and stay with them after college, and I appreciate that, but I have other plans.

The North Pole isn't all it's cracked up to be, especially for someone that isn't always chipper and hoping for peace on earth. I simply want a little of the latter for myself. This town is magical because of what it is and who lives in it, but under the toys, candy canes, and tinsels, the same issues that plague everyone else still exist. My father and mother are proof of that.

They had a shotgun wedding at my grandfather's decree when he found out his just turned legal daughter was knocked up, something they threw in each other's faces every chance they got, not giving a shit I knew I was the catalyst to their misery. As the story goes, my grandpa, Leroy Smith, was one of the best welders here. He wasn't leaving, and he refused to let my parents leave either, so every day I had to hear how much better their lives would've been if they'd been able to move instead of having to give up their dreams.

Within seconds of me getting out of here, I'm sure they'll be doing the same. Minding my own business, I walk the streets toward home. We live in the less glamorous part of town which is still nicer than it would be in other parts of the world. It has four bedrooms, a white picket fence, and is in mint condition, yet by the standards here, we're average working family. Which never ceases to piss my mother off, as she'd been part of the glitzier neighborhood growing up. However, since my father has no ambition, according to her, we're stuck in poverty, a sentiment which causes me to roll my eyes at her. She's never worked a day in her life, claiming she's a stay-at-home mom. Ha! I spent as many hours as possible with the Claus' or at Molly Jones' house, the mom of John Alexander, my other best friend. There are even pictures of me as a baby with the Claus children during the holidays instead of being at my house.

I'm so lost in thought I don't hear the bike until it's upon me, and I almost trip in my hurry to avoid it running me over. "Freak!" The rider screams before the feel of liquid hits me. *Are you fucking serious?*

Troy 'the asshole' Dawson, my biggest tormentor since elementary school. He's nineteen yet refuses to act his age. Glancing at my black dress, goth wear being my preference, I'm thankful to note you can't see what I realize was soda. Unfortunately, some of it seeped into my black combat boots, and my *Manic Panic* purple dye is now dripping from my hair and staining my skin. That pisses me off and I make a mental note to get him back prior to leaving.

Reaching my house, the scene playing out on the front lawn startles me. My parents are arguing in broad daylight as Dad, luggage in hand, is getting smacked on the chest by my mom. Sadly, that doesn't surprise me as it's nothing new. What does is the fact it's happening in front of our neighbors. That is unheard of, they usually hide it for the sake of appearances. For years, we've been whispered about, no one daring to discuss us out loud. That's not to say I haven't caught plenty talking shit regarding us, though.

I open the gate, ignoring everyone's stares and try to control the situation. "What the fuck are you doing?" I scream, causing both pairs of eyes to shoot my direction. They immediately shut their mouths, but it doesn't last long before mom blurts out something I was hoping would wait until after I left.

"Your father is leaving me for another woman. Now that you're an adult, he has no use for us. And I gave him the best years of my life." Her tears might sway those watching, having them viewing her as the innocent and injured party, but I know better. They're both guilty.

"No, you didn't. I was forced to marry you, Kelly. To have a child neither of us wanted, but at least it came with an expiration date. Chelsea is eighteen and now I'm fucking free." Then he looks at me, and instead of saying good-bye, I'll see you later, or anything similar, he states, "Good luck with that train wreck."

I should be sad as he goes, his lack of regret at leaving me behind certainly would make any child want to cry, but not me. I turn my back on him and face the woman I now have to deal with and remind myself it's only for a few more hours.

"Chelsea, sweetie, what are we going to do? He was my world. He provided for us. How will we survive without him?" She drops to her knees and clings to my legs, and purple dye begins to seep into her blonde hair that is so much like my own natural color. I glance around, noticing the cowards that were so interested now running away that the show is over.

"Get up, mom," I tell her, unable to bring myself to comfort her. A part of me feels awful at being so harsh, but another just doesn't fucking give a crap any longer. At the realization she won't get the pity she wants from me, nor the neighbors as they're all gone, she does. Wiping the crocodile tears off her face, she walks inside the house as I stand there alone, wet, and cold, despite the summer breeze. Minutes tick by before I find the energy to move, and when I do, I head to my room, ready to finish packing the couple things left, then sleep off this horrible night.

Except the next morning, things don't go as planned. The first inclination something is wrong is the clattering of metal and men yelling *Green Day* shirt, then gather my hair in a messy bun on top of my head as an afterthought.

Movers are milling about, putting things in boxes while my grandfather stands next to my mom and directs everyone. He doesn't even bother to hide the disdain that crosses his face when he notices me. Then man has never cared for me and I know it. *Get in line, dude.*

"Say hi to your grandpa," mom suggests in a voice that does not belong to a grown-ass woman. I vow to not let anything get to me as I move closer.

"Chelsea, you appear well," he greets me, oozing insincerity.

"And you're…alive," I reply, unable to resist.

"Young lady!" I roll my eyes at her fake outrage, tired of this charade.

"No need, pumpkin. She is half his daughter, so she couldn't inherit all your good qualities. However, she'll be taught manners soon enough." He takes a step, trying to intimidate me I'm sure, unaware it has no impact on me. "Remove all that crap you call fashion and try to look like a normal person your age before you come to my house."

I stand taller, straighten my shoulders, and stare him in the eyes. "I will not be stepping foot in your home. I have my ticket out of here and I'm using it."

"Good, then get your shit and go," he replies harshly, and at the bottom of my already cold soul, though I'll never admit it, it burns. I run upstairs and grab my bags which contain nothing more than the necessities as I do not want any reminders of this place. Thanks to almost twenty thousand from my favorite aunt on my dad's side, I have leeway for a while. She was everything I aspired to be, and an artist that lived to the fullest. Never having any children of her own, she'd have me spend the summer with her sometimes, showing me that life could be in color, not the black and white everyone claimed it had to be. She, too, had been an outcast, labeled the weird one in her family, and refused to let fear stop her from doing what she wanted.

Her death was the only time I've ever cried. Aunt Lydia didn't have much, but what she did, she left to me. No one else received anything, not even a letter. I got the money and a video, one that brings me to tears every time I see it. Apparently, she'd been sick a while and had gone to the mountains to enjoy her last months as she pleased. Her message gave me the courage to leave now. Her instructions were direct and clear, giving me the courage to do as she told me to – take the money she bequeathed to me and run as far from my parents as possible. She said to follow my dream and never let others dictate my life.

Not even bothering to tell them bye, I walk outside and hop on my scooter to head toward the bank. There's a line as I'd expected when I arrive since it's payday. The tellers always take too long to deal with a single customer, their over the top necessity for excellence often making a quick transaction into a ten-minute ordeal. I'd been here before with my dad and waited over two hours. Of course, here in the jolly North Pole, no one but me seems to mind. I'd prepared for this possibility and decided to take the five o'clock trolley out of here, which gives me plenty of time. A half hour later, I'm next.

"Ms. McQueen, it's nice to see you. What may I do for you?" The young teller asks. I recognize her from a few days ago when I came to make sure everything would be in order.

"Hi. I've come to make the transaction we spoke about, and to close my account as well." A look of confusion, then apprehension moves over her face, though the smile never leaves her lips, and I know once again that something is wrong. She excuses herself and hurries to the side door where the branch manager sits all day unless there's trouble. When she points at me, I start to chew my nails, growing more nervous by the moment. Finally, she returns and asks me to follow her, and she takes me to the office she'd just left. When she disappears, the door closing behind her, I shift to look at the guy wearing the same expression and smile as she was. He verifies my name, then tugs on his tie as if it's suddenly choking him a bit, before folding his hands in front of him on the desk. He clears his throat, even sips a bit of his water, all while I wait to hear what bullshit policy he'll try to throw at me. I'm sure they don't want me to remove all that money, but they can't stop me. It's mine, and I'm of age.

"I'd appreciate it if you could hurry as I have a trolley to catch."

"Um… about that Ms. McQueen." I hold up my hand, halting his protest, and assure him I know it isn't safe to hide it under a mattress as opposed to within his establishment, and that isn't my intention. I'm only withdrawing it as I'm leaving town. "That's not it at all. There are just no funds to give you." I blink rapidly, sure there's a punchline, though this is not a funny joke at all, but it never comes.

He proceeds to tell me he's sorry, and that my dad emptied my account the day prior to me turning eighteen, and that he'd been allowed to do so as the power of attorney until I was legal. I punch the desk so hard my hand starts bleeding, and at some point, and I remember very little after his bomb, the Clauses are called. They take me to the clinic for treatment, and the second I'm pronounced free to go, I take off.

"Chels! Hold up!" Brandie shouts, John Alexander on her heels. They came as soon as they heard, and I love them for that, but I need to be alone. The realization I'm stuck where I'm different from everybody else is hitting hard.

My dream crashed and burned, and I don't even have a place to lay my head. I rush to my scooter, thankful someone brought it here, and ride, uncaring that it's dark and we're not allowed to be out this far. I flee for my usual spot by the mountains, needing to clear my head.

It's not as if my life can get any worse, right?

Chapter Three

~ Chels ~

Present day…

"Mr. Johnson, I fixed the sink. Tell your children to stop putting plastic forks down the dispenser so this doesn't keep happening. I'll be back later to fix Timmy's computer. I know you don't wanna hear this, but this is the third time this month. I think you have a teenage porn-watching problem, and that leads to viruses," I inform him as I get up, then wipe my hands on the rag I keep in my back pocket.

He comes closer, looks over his shoulder for his wife first, then states, "I've told his ass to stop." He pulls out his wallet and hands me four crisp hundred-dollar bills, telling me, "This should cover both repairs. All I ask is that my poor wife doesn't hear about what he's been doing." I shake his hand as I promise not to say a word, then thank him, letting him know he paid me more than necessary. "It's the least I could do. I know how hard you work around here." He hesitates a moment and I know what's coming, the pity party everyone throws when I come around. I hate it, but they've known me my whole life, so I can't truly get mad at them.

"Your mama's been asking for you, said she'd like to see you."

"I'll think about it, okay?" I ask, forcing a smile that I know doesn't fool him, and we're each simply giving the expected response. I haven't seen her in over five years and that was only in passing at the grocery store where she tried to stop me, but I kept walking. I don't let gossip ruin my life, though I did hear that she's now happily married, and they had a little girl, who was on her hip that day, within a couple years of dad splitting. Good for her is my thought on both. Maybe she won't regret having this child like she did me.

Looking at my watch, I realize I'm running late and rush outside to jump on the trusty scooter I've had since high school. I just need it to make it through the next couple weeks. After parking, I take the stairs two at a time to the small studio I rent from Molly.

Checking my clothes with a quick sniff, I know there's no way I can meet the guy paying me to pretend to be his girlfriend smelling like this. Fixing my appearance wouldn't be a bad idea either. I ignore the barks of my only companion, fully aware if I stop to play, I'll never want to leave because I always give in to the fluffy thing. Once all that is taken care of, I work on calming my nerves, going so far as to give myself a pep talk as I look at my reflection in the bathroom mirror. "You can do this." I adjust my black frames, thankful they hide the hazel eyes somewhat, though I wish it was more. I hate the color because I inherited them from my piece of shit father.

I couldn't do much about them, unfortunately, not like I do with my hair that still reminds me of my mom, wearing it any way I can to be different from her. As evidenced by the dreadlocks I gather into a ponytail. It's not exactly warm outside, but I'm only going downstairs, so I reach for my shorts and an oversized hoodie, already anxious to get this over with. In less than twenty minutes, I'll be meeting a man prepared to pay me the final thousand I need to finally get out of this town, a decade later than I'd hoped.

When you're a teen, you can't imagine life seeming to pass in what feels like a blink of an eye, but it does. One day you're full of hope, dreams, and aspirations, and the next you're almost thirty with a bad knee, drawing a blank on what you had for breakfast. *Adulting sucks ass and anyone who tells you different is smoking the good shit.*

I didn't even have a steady job per se, choosing instead to become the town handywoman instead of working for the Claus family who owns everything except for a few places. They wanted me to make up with my mom due to their preference of trying to see the good in everyone, but I don't share that philosophy. Thankfully, my talent for being able to learn by merely watching others came in handy, and it keeps me pretty busy as there is always something needing my attention. The downside is that I don't make much, as I can't charge the same as those who actually studied their respective trade. With this "business arrangement," I'll have a total of six grand saved, giving me a tiny security blanket to fund my escape.

I know it's wrong, but I can't help the fact I have a mental image of a lanky guy with glasses like mine and a voice so faint you can barely hear him, and my heart hurts for him. I know what it's like to be lonely having regularly been referred to as either a spinster or cat lady. Ironically, I have a dog, though her name is Kat, short for Katrine. Of course, I'd gotten her after one too many jokes thrown my way, my version of thumbing my nose at them. Kat is my ride or die girl and will be the only thing I take with me from this life.

Speaking of, my adoring Kat stares at me when I open the door, sad she's staying home while I run out. I kneel and pet behind her ears, smiling as she tilts, telling me she wants more. Kissing the top of her head, I promise her treats when I get back, then lock the door and take the stairs to the restaurant below. I want to arrive a few minutes early to settle myself. Especially because I know I'll be awkward as I haven't dated in so fucking long. Hell, my trusty vibe, Jack, is all I need in my opinion as far as what men can do for me.

I'd asked John to let the guy know I'd be at the last booth, so I get comfortable in that spot, thanking Molly for the shake she insists on giving me on the house. All these years later, she still tries to take care of me. While I wait, I nervously tap my foot under the granite table. Tony, Molly's husband, just renovated the place to resemble a diner from the fifties. I love the decor, finding it artsier than the usual Christmas themes that cover the whole town. The music, however, is from the eighties, and my head starts bobbing to it. Prince and Stevie Nicks never fail to put me in a good mood.

Right on time, the bell jingles and I peer up to find a huge guy. That can't be him, so there's no use engaging in eye contact with a stranger. Maybe he stood you up? *Wouldn't that be my luck, to have a person that needs to pay for a date do that?* Standing, intent on getting some air, I bump against what feels like a solid wall, the massive chest of the man I'd just dismissed.

"Watch it!" I yell as I land on my ass in the seat I'd just vacated. Thank goodness I wore shorts. Propping myself up on my elbows, I take a good glance at the giant idiot and my breath catches a bit. He's hot and dangerous looking. He's got bad news written all over him, the opposite of what you find around here. He's well over six feet of packed muscles encased in jeans and a dress shirt with sleeves rolled up. Tattoos cover his arms and the skin revealed due to the first few buttons being undone. My body responds, and I curse the fact I'm attracted to some man with a mobster vibe while I'm here to meet another.

"Sorry about that, sweetie. I didn't mean to startle you," he apologizes. "Let me help." His deep voice adds to the attraction. As if he can read my thoughts, a smile appears, though it seems foreign to him, and of course, it makes him even sexier. His ash blond hair is slicked back, but a strand escapes, giving me the urge to mess the rest up, and his emerald eyes hint at darkness. When his big hand wraps around mine, something short circuits, warning me to put distance between us now. I attempt to snatch my hand from him, though he hesitates to release it.

"If you'll excuse me, I'm waiting for my date. He'll be here any minute," I inform him.

Chapter Four

~ Romeo ~

I wish I could cancel this whole charade, and I haven't even entered the damn restaurant yet. Not that I wasn't tempted to do so within seconds of agreeing to John's idea. However, I had let him state that I was dating a friend of his in front of my mom at my sister's rehearsal dinner, so I was well and truly fucked if I didn't continue down this path. Yes, I'm a grown-ass man, and this is a desperate act for the son of Lovin. My mom is the most notorious Cupid and has become more intent on pairing me off the past decade. I'm the only single offspring left, my sister tying the knot within a week, despite it being to a man she barely knows.

She appears content, but we're close and I know better. This is a sham. I know she's pining for Dr. Lantern, though he doesn't return her feelings due to her age. That's the only reason I haven't killed him, that being said, at this point I'd much rather she be with him instead of a loveless marriage. Not even my refusal to accept the engagement put a halt to this absurdity. I need to find a way to stop it, and that can only happen if our mom got off my back. Hence, agreeing to John's plan.

The place is empty, which is why I chose it. I couldn't imagine any woman wanting an audience when they were literally selling themselves. Yes, it's only as a companion, but it bothers me that she feels she has to do this. Especially here, where everyone has a good life.

Genevieve is my aunt on my dad's side. Being a Cupid and choosing to go Claus created quite the uproar, but she's one of the few that never cared for tradition. John and his husband, Kent, are why I only occasionally come here as I prefer the warmer climate of my hometown.

Taking a moment to adjust to the dim light, they instantly zoom in on the small frame at the table I was instructed to use. All I can make out under the huge hoodie is a tall yet petite body. I'm ready to bolt, taking the fact that I don't see my "date," as a sign, when the most gorgeous face I've ever seen glances my way for a mere second. I'm drawn to her like a magnet to a metal forcefield, my body pushing forward until I'm in front of her. A swirl of emotion stirs where she bumped into me, and I fucking know I'm never letting her go. Her gorgeous hazel eyes inspect me, her reaction showing that she's equally affected.

A million indecent thoughts flood my mind, all involving the undoubtedly sweet pussy covered by her tight shorts, when she falls back to the seat. I want to see the rest of that sexy little body she keeps hidden, as well as the black ink I spy under the hoodie. First, I need to get rid of whoever John is sending as there's now only one woman I want at my side. She can't be John's friend. She's too gorgeous, too mine to offer herself up like that.

When she informs me she's there for a date, I want nothing more than to break the fucker's neck. ""The fuck you are," I growl, worried my gruff demeanor will shock her. It doesn't. She merely stands, putting her flush against me. She's tall, but still shorter than my height of six-five. There's fire in her stare, and while I can tell she's attracted to me, that doesn't mean she won't also give me hell.

"That's none of your business. Get out of here, okay?"

Ignoring her uninformative answer, I lean closer, ensuring she'll need to crane her neck to hold my gaze. "What's your name, sweetheart?" The roll of her eyes at the endearment eggs me on, and I know I'll be calling her that for the rest of our lives.

"If it will make you retreat, I'll tell you. I'm Chelsea, but I go by Chels. Satisfied? Now can you please leave? You'll fuck up my ticket out of here."

This is her? How the fuck has no man swept this woman up, married her, and demanded she never leaves their sight ever again? The fact they haven't means I'm a lucky bastard. Then what she said hits me. She wants out of here, going so far as to accept money from a stranger. I know that's me, and I don't give a fuck that I'm suddenly jealous of my own damn self. I try to calm down before I continue, knowing she'd fight if I followed through on my instinct of carrying her from here, after spanking her ass for agreeing to this, then have the first priest I see marry us. I can have her tied to me forever in a matter of hours.

"Romeo Cupid Junior, your date." And then I give a showy bow, hiding my smirk as her scowl falters a bit until she stammers that I can't be.

"You're not a short balding man that's shy and socially awkward."

"Sorry to disappoint you. How about we get to know each other? It'll give me a chance to see if you're the right fit for the job." I have to stifle my laugh as her eyes burn with a fire that would obliterate me if she could. I'm going to love making this woman mad. The makeup sex alone will be worth it.

"I don't fucking need this. You should've asked your questions beforehand, asshole." She pushes at me, but I don't move an inch. I may like poking at her, but when Molly begins coming toward us, wanting to know if everything is all right, I know this isn't the time. "I suggest you sit down. I'd hate to have to tell her why we're here." Her face turns every shade of red, and I wonder if the rest of her is, too. Arms folded across her chest, Chels tells Molly it is through gritted teeth. Thankfully, she leaves, but I can feel her watching us. "Give me your hand."

"Why? You're a jackass."

"Molly is getting suspicious, and we can only hold her off for so long. We can either play this as a lover's spat or tell her the truth. The lunch rush is about to start and I doubt you want everyone knowing your business." I must hit the nerve as she lays her hand in mine, and I take the opportunity to place a kiss to the back of it. "It's a pleasure to meet you, Ms. McQueen." I don't release her, instead choosing to rub slow circles on her wrists which seems to soothe her.

"Can we get this over with? Just tell me where to be and when. I also expect payment in cash and upfront. I'm not getting screwed."

"There's only one way I want to do that, and it involves you being a lot more pleasant and pliant." I deserve the kick in the balls she gives me, and I'll be damned if it doesn't turn me on. Apparently, I'm a masochist where this woman is concerned.

"The only pliant thing will be your dick when I cut it and wear it as a trophy!"

"Hey, as long as it's somewhere near you, I'm happy," I inform her, my voice a decibel higher than normal.

"Are you always this annoying? I can see why you have to pay a woman if you are. If it was any other man, I'd go through with this, but I don't think I can deal with you. I'm sure I can find a different desperate guy that needs a date."

"The fucking you will."

She stands, slamming both hands on the table, and her next words hurt worse than the kick to my junk. "For all you know, I could have one. Perhaps this is a side hustle, and you're merely another client." My brain is telling me I'm being unreasonable, and I know she's lying, but my heart is climbing from my chest. The blood pumping through my veins is heated and this imaginary guy is already six feet underground.

If I'm honest, the fucking need to have her confirm she's just messing with me propels me to keep going, and I don't give a shit how irrational that sounds. Rising, I know tower over her and declare, "Angel, no man in their right mind would let you parade that sassy ass of yours in this town, nor making private meetings with strange men. I know that for a fucking fact. If I was your man, I'd be sniffing every single inch of the North Pole like a hound dog, and my nose would always lead me to wherever that sweet pussy of yours goes." The small tremble of her hand has me feeling victorious, but I do admire her tenacity. She closes her eyes a second in what I can assume is an attempt to center herself, then opens them and entrances me.

"But you ain't my man, are ya? You're just a Stupid Cupid." Without missing a beat, I pull her to me by the back of her neck, causing her to go to her tiptoes to maintain her balance.

"For the next week, I am, and you can bet your sweet ass I'm following that delicious scent all over this fucking town." I ravish her mouth before she can say another word, and the first taste of her decadent lips is as sweet as the finest chocolate. The moan that escapes is so faint she probably doesn't even know she did it, but the sound might as well be an orchestra.

It resonates in my eardrums, but the minute I hear a few men come in, I force myself to stop. If I don't, I'll end up killing a fucker simply because he got to hear her breathe. Reluctantly, I pull away, self-preservation the only thing giving me the strength to do so as I can't end up in jail minutes after finding the woman I will now obsess over day and night. It physically hurts to let her go as I want her mouth again, her scent on my skin, her screaming my name as I take her.

The thought alone has me readjusting my hard dick for the hundredth time since laying eyes on her. We need to get her out of here now. Somehow all the men have been too blind to see how gorgeous she is up to this point, but I'm not taking a risk that'll change. "Let's go, angel. We'll hit the bank, and then go somewhere more private to discuss the details."

She looks around and notices there are a few people staring at us and nods her agreement. I throw a hundred on the table even though we didn't order because I can tell Molly cares for my girl. There's not enough money in the world to repay her for that, though I'm going to try. I have a feeling Chels has a lot of secrets and doesn't let anyone close, but she did for Molly, and that has to mean something.

I intend to join that exclusive list, and I only have a week to do it.

Chapter Five
~ Chels ~

Okay, I was not expecting a kiss like that, nor have I ever had one that comes close. Yeah, I've had boyfriends, even a couple lovers, but Romeo's mouth was perfectly in sync with mine, as if we'd done it a thousand times. No man had ever dared tell me how things were gonna be, fully aware I'd beat his ass and leave the fucker crying. Romeo, though, not only took my kick to his junk like a pro, but then laid a smooch on me as if he had…enjoyed it?

That turned every single cell in my body on and had me wanting to climb him then and there. Something about his presence told me I was entering the devil's lair, but I didn't care. I'm fucking thankful I decided to go with the hoodie, saved me from sporting an embarrassingly big wet spot.

When he asks me to follow him, I'm still dazed and unsure exactly how I feel, and decide to not fight him on this. Plus, I could use the fresh air, so he and I aren't in such close quarters. I watch him throw money on the table and almost stop him, but he gives me a look that warns me against it. I once more find myself complying, though I try to tell myself it's because the cash will go to Molly, and she definitely deserves it. Honestly, I like that he did it, even hoping it'll make a painful dent in his wallet. Then again, he's willing to pay me a grand down for a date, so I highly doubt he'll feel the loss. I'm so engrossed in my thoughts, I don't see him reach for me nor his intent to intertwine our fingers, until it's done, his grip airtight. Telling me without words I'm not getting away unless he allows it.

"Don't, princess. I'm holding your hand because we need to get used to each other if we want others to believe this."

"I wasn't going to, smartass."

"That's better than dumbass, so I'll take it!" His panty-melting smile appears, and I curse myself for getting into this mess. I can't make it worse, meaning I need to stay out of his bed. If he fucks as he kisses, I'm in big trouble. A few more patrons start pouring in, making me thankful we're leaving as I know everything I do gets reported to my asshole grandfather. I do not need him knowing who Romeo is. He's already smeared my name because I refused to take part in their facade.

"Shit!" Romeo curses under his breath as he seems to search his pockets.

"Everything okay?"

"I left my glasses. Wait right here." I nod, knowing full well I'm walking out that door the second he turns his head because I need a moment. I can't think when he's near me with those green eyes and god-like body. Exiting, I move toward the stairwell and lean against it, watching as one of the assembly-line workers, makes his way to me. I'd forgotten the plumbing job at his house, my meeting with Romeo obviously taking longer than I'd assumed it would.

"Herman, I'm sorry. It slipped my mind," I say, adding an excuse so he doesn't pry.

"No worries, babe. I get it. Can you please come by around eight, though? I need you. I have to work late, but you know where the keys are to let yourself…" Before he can finish his sentence, he's lifted by a very angry Romeo and thrown into the wall. My eyes pop out of their socket at the action. The fucking man is insane.

"What the hell are you asking my woman to do at your house that fucking late?" Romeo growls, letting me know I need to stop this. Poor Herman is half his size and is already turning blue. Even if he wanted to answer and defend himself, he wouldn't be able to.

"I'm fixing his pipe."

"Mother fucker! Now I'm going to hurt you!" Damn. It's then I realize that was not a good choice as an explanation. I tug his arm, trying to get through to him. "I'm the fucking plumber. Let him go before his wife comes. Becca is a cop and will throw your ass in jail!"

"Plumber, wife…" He doesn't sound convinced, but he must realize I'm telling the truth. As soon as he lets go, Herman runs like the wind.

"Never mind, Chels. I can do it myself," he shouts as he disappears. I have a feeling he'll never request my services again, which makes me pissed at Romeo, especially the part about him calling me his woman. Even if my body reacted to his display and I'm having issues breathing because it hit something deep inside I didn't know was there. Going with anger, which allows me to avoid exploring these damn feelings, I smack him. He doesn't even flinch as his eyes focus on me, danger coming off him in waves.

"What the hell are you doing in the homes of strange men at night? Is that something you do often?" He asks, his firm hold keeping me in place. I could easily break free as he's not hurting me, but all I want to do is yell at him. This isn't going to end well. There will be fighting and screaming, just like my parents. Things will no doubt get volatile between us, and that will cause some damage. I have to run as far as I can.

"Frankly, it's none of your business. You need to learn about boundaries. My life is private. You can't scare off my clients like that. Our arrangement is only for a fucking week."

"And I will know anything I fucking want to about you in that week."

"I'm done. A thousand isn't enough for this headache." I push his hands off me, his touch seeming to burn my skin in their absence. *What the hell has gotten into me?* I need this money, but I will not let him use it to blackmail me. I'll earn it another way.

"A hundred thousand in cash now." That life-changing amount stops me in my tracks. There's no fucking way I heard him right. I turn back slowly, hiding my shock at his offer, though my mind is listing all the things I can do with it. A down payment on a house, a sensible car, and perhaps a little shop. I'd be set for the first few years.

"Are you serious?"

"Yes, but I ask, you answer truthfully. If I want you to do something within reason, you do it. And no, I don't mean sex." I admit that was where my mind had gone, and I should be relieved at his clarification, but something deep inside me actually hates that it's not part of the deal. The turmoil has me wanting to lash out, and that side seems saner.

"So, I'm supposed to be your trophy, a piece of ass for sale. Sure, I'll just sit still and look pretty while doing as I'm told."

"For fuck sake. That's not what I want, and you know it." His face transforms into disgust. "I want you to be you because that's what makes you so damn enticing. I simply need to know you won't hide things from me. Is that so hard to understand? What's the worst that could happen? I spoil you a bit, buy you a few dresses, and get to know the real you? You intrigue me, Chels, more than anything ever has." He rakes his hand over his face, visibly frustrated. "Damn it, woman. You're maddening and outspoken. You give me shit, kick me in the balls, and slap me when I cross the line. And that's just in the last hour. I'm fucking addicted to it. I can't explain it, which is saying a lot given my profession, but I need it. Grace me with your presence, even if only for a week."

He steps forward, wrapping a dreadlock around his finger, and pleads, "Let me be your man without a protest every second, let me to show you how you should be treated because it sure isn't you how you have been. All I'm asking is for you to trust me a little."

Biting my lip, I mull it over. I can do this, then take my cash and run. I've dealt with assholes my whole life, at least this one is nice to look at. But trust? With the exception of a couple people, whenever I'd given it, they'd ripped it to shreds. It's why I stay in my own corner.

"Half a million if you agree right now", he blurts out when I fail to answer right away.

"That's too much. I can't...that's a fortune." He has to be fucking with me.

"You're worth every penny. It'll probably take the bank a few days, but I'm sure I can get a big chunk of it now. Might not be safe to carry that much on you."

"I don't know what to say."

"Yes, that's all I need." The second I give it to him, the edges of his mouth curve. I just made a deal with the devil. He yanks me to him and kisses me, his tongue slipping past my lips as he takes control. I'm pressed so tightly against his sculpted body I can feel his heart racing, the rhythm almost hypnotizing me. The bulge in his pants is not small by any means, and when he drags his hand down my spine, goosebumps cover me.

My senses are trying to play catch up, but he owns every single one and is using them to maneuver me to his will, that's the only thing I can think of to explain the ache in the pit of my stomach. He doesn't release me until I'm gasping for air. Needing some kind of distance, I remind him he said sex isn't part of the deal. "It isn't, sweetheart, but I never said I wouldn't touch what now belongs to me." He kisses my forehead, the sweet gesture such a contrast to the other which was a mark of ownership.

"We might as well have been fucking," I snap.

"Believe me, that wasn't anything near what I want to do to you. I haven't started showing you just how good I can make you feel. You'll be begging me to fuck you all on your own, and once that happens…you won't want to leave my side."

"Cockiness isn't attractive," I warn him, fully aware it's not a great comeback, but it's hard to think when he's threatening me with mind-blowing sex.

"We'll see."

"We will when I put my foot up your ass."

"Ooh, dirty talk." I roll my eyes at him as we walk to the bank in silence and his arm possessively settles over my shoulders. It takes all my concentration to keep my breathing normal, so I'm thankful when we arrive. Unfortunately, he doesn't let me go as he does the paperwork as I'd hoped. After an hour of dealing with the manager who continually flicked a glance at me, Romeo not so kindly reminded him to keep his gaze on his computer unless he wanted to lose his sight forever. He listened, and it wasn't long before we were out of there.

"I have big plans for tomorrow and they require a few calls, so we need to get going," he says, giving my ass a quick swat. Admittedly, I had spaced out. In my defense, though, I do have a quarter of a million in my bag, and the knowledge that the rest will be available in two days.

"Sorry. Can you repeat that?"

"Where do you live? I want to make sure you get home safely. Also, I gotta get some clothes for you to wear before I go crazy. Those shorts look like fucking panties."

"I live upstairs from Molly's restaurant, and I'll have you know these are my work shorts."

"Not for much fucking longer. You live there by yourself?

"Yeah, why? Let me guess, you have a problem with that, too?"

"Damn right! Pack an overnight bag, you're staying with me. We'll consider it me protecting my investment." And then he has the audacity to wink, and I curl my fist, forcing myself not to smack him again.

"No. I'm a grown-ass woman and will be fine on my own. No need to play knight in shining armor all week. I've done just fine without you."

"I disagree. You're the one taking on dates-for-hire for extra cash." That pierces a part of me I never let anyone get near, and I hate him for speaking the truth I didn't want to face. If my parents had cared for me at all, I would've managed better. If I hadn't been so naive where they were concerned, I would've been savvier. Being confronted by these realizations by a complete stranger catches me off guard and I have to blink back a tear. This isn't me, not any longer. I did all my crying the day my dream was taken from me. Everything after that is on me, and that's a fact I have to live with.

"Shit, I'm sorry. I shouldn't have said that. Please, forgive me." He reaches out, but I flinch, fearing his touch will only add to it. I'm not fragile and I don't need anyone's pity, especially his. He doesn't stop me as I hurry to get away, but he doesn't leave either, just merely slows his pace. When I get to my destination, he stops and watches me go inside. I can see him standing there when I look out of my window, and he glances up, as if he knows I'm there. There's a storm brewing inside him, his eyes so full of emotion as they gaze at me tells me so, but I can't let myself think of how vulnerable he just made me feel.

After he finally leaves, I collapse on the floor in relief. I didn't think he'd go, and I'm still surprised that he did. He has to be up to something. Romeo does not strike me as a man that gives up that easily.

That fact is confirmed an hour later when a car bearing the logo of one of the private securities in town parks outside, facing my door.

Fucker.

Chapter Six

~ Romeo ~

I've been so busy trying to talk to my sister and deal with my mom who is bat shit crazier than usual that I haven't seen my angel in almost two days. I did call her, though she screamed at me as I'd apparently sent her too many gifts. I can see how the five-carat princess cut ring I insisted she wear might've been overkill, but in my defense, I wanted it to be bigger than that. My restraint should be applauded. Of course, it wasn't needed at all. However, Chels doesn't know that part. Needing an excuse to get it on her I may have told her my mom thinks we're engaged, and by the time she learns differently, I hope she's already fallen for me.

My game plan for the day is to charm her with pampering, buying her everything she's always wanted, and a special surprise later. If my friends and family saw me now, they'd assume that I'd gone insane. They all know me as the man determined to remain a bachelor, and here I am essentially trying to trap someone I just met. While it could've looked as if I was avoiding relationships to piss my mom off, I merely refused to settle for less than my soulmate.

The Cupid heritage makes you more receptive to your own emotions, meaning dating had become mundane, not to mention futile as it always left me feeling empty and alone. At this point, I figured I'd remain single forever, but one look at Chelsea and I was done. Now I need her to get on the same page because I'll never stop chasing her. She's mine, and I'll spend the rest of my days making sure she understands she's my first priority from here on out.

Glancing at my watch for the third time, I see she's running late, which is rare for her from what I've discovered, and I start to panic until I see her scooter. She's adorable in a flannel shirt with the sleeves rolled up, a vest over that, cowboy boots, and once again shorts that are barely there. Her cleavage gives me the opportunity to see that she's also braless, making me curse under my breath. She's a fucking wet dream come to life. If I wasn't determined to make her feel special in other ways…There's apprehension in her step as she nears the front door, and I'm sure she's tempted to leave, so I run to the door.

"Where are you going, sweetheart? Trying to back out already?"

"I just haven't been to this store in a long time. I don't have the best memories here." Her expression as she glances at the place has me on alert. She enters instead of offering more information, and I make a mental note to look into it late.

"Are you okay? Do you want to go somewhere else?"

"It's fine. Let's just get this over with."

She takes my hand when I extend it, allowing me to see the ring on her finger where it belongs, and I can't resist placing a kiss above it. "I haven't been able to feast on your beauty in way too long for my liking." She rolls her eyes, but I'm serious. I missed her and can't hold myself back another minute. With my palm at the center of her back, I pull her against me. The action startles her, and she has to lean on me when she loses her footing. I curse myself for wearing my suit today. If I'd gone causal, there'd be fewer layers keeping her from me.

"I knew you couldn't resist me for long," I say, knowing it'll rile her up. She attempts to swat me, but I catch her wrist and lay it on my chest, then push it over my abs and down to the bulge in my pants. Starved for her, I hiss at the contact, knowing her light touch could make me jizz like a schoolboy with a couple strokes. She doesn't tense up nor stop me, but a playful smile curls her lips as she runs her tongue over the bottom one.

"What's the matter, big boy? Did I leave you with aching balls last time?" She squeezes me and I close my eyes, concentrating on not coming in the high-end boutique.

"I tossed and turned for hours, hating how cold the bed was without you. If you would've agreed to come home with me, you would've been screaming my name all night. This is all for you, baby. You do this to me. I convinced John to send me a picture of you and stroked myself over and over while visualizing you were there with me."

"Is that so? Was I nice?" She wants to know, her grip turning almost punishing. "Did I give you hell? Scratch you while you thrust into me? Tell me, Ro, what did you dirty mind have me doing?" Her calling me a nickname no one else ever has makes me lose control. Her soft lips would make any man beg for more, and I thank my lucky stars I'm the only one that has that right from now on. I slide my tongue inside when she opens for me, showing her this ownership is fucking mutual. The way we're devouring each other borders on sexual, I can feel cum dripping from my dick and running down my leg. I'll have a hard-on the rest of the day, and we haven't even gotten to the clothes fitting yet.

"Ahem." The clearing of a throat interrupts us, and we break apart, both breathing hard. Her eyes gaze into my soul, shield fully back in place, warning me the playful side has retreated. She's too late, though. I'm now on a mission to have that version whenever we're together.

"Mr. Cupid, I assume? My assistant filled me in. Had it been a few weeks ago, I would've been swamped, but I hope you realize the big favor I'm granting you as it's such short notice." I wouldn't normally care what anyone thinks, nor that she won't shake my hand as is polite, but I don't like how my angel started acting since she appeared.

"Thank you. You will be compensated for your time; of that I can assure you. Now if you can show me and my fiancée where the clothes are?" She quickly masks her shock at the title, but I saw it nonetheless. We follow her as asked, but my woman has become a version of herself that I do not care for, and it's pissing me off. I ask her to go while Chels tries on the wardrobe I'd requested to be laid out for her, but she doesn't do so until I threaten to call my aunt.

Chels visibly relaxes, a rush of air leaves her the second we're alone, proving that I'd made the right choice. Thankfully, after a few jokes, Chels is her usual feisty self, and even enjoys putting on a show. A lot of the outfits the woman chose aren't what I'd picture my Chels selecting, but she's a good sport and tries them on, too. She exits the dressing room seductively, then sashays toward me. It's meant to make me laugh but makes me fucking hard. The last one is a fucking masterpiece. A short skirt paired with an off-the-shoulder top accentuates her gorgeous body, and makes her legs look a mile long.

"What's the matter? Can't take all these curves coming at you?" Then she gives a little beat, inserting "boom chicka wow wow."

"You come any closer in that little number, I doubt the owner will like the consequences," I warn her, and the laugh that earns me is so sweet and honest. I have a feeling she hasn't done that in a long time.

"The uptight bitty would banish us for life. Having to see your thingy might actually be worth pissing her off."

"Ouch. Did you forgot you were massaging it outside?"

"Must not have been that memorable." I growl at her response, then stomp closer, satisfied at the blush creeping up her cheeks. I lift her, forcing her legs to wrap around my waist and her skirt to bunch up. The only thing between us is her thong and my zipper.

"Let's see if I can trigger your memory." Her chocolate and espresso scent surrounds me, and I draw it in. I know she'll be a hellcat in my bed, and not for the first time, I wonder if she'll dig her nails in my skin, scratching me as she insinuated. Or is she a biter? Visions of her sweet and sassy mouth on my shoulder as her teeth dig in while I'm balls deep pushes me over the edge.

"I'm. Fucking. Done," I vow with heated kisses. "You're fucking mine. Your mouth, your body, and this pussy is mine." Her breathing becomes labored when I thrust my hips forward, and the little noises she starts making only furthers my already insane possessiveness where she's concerned. I couldn't care less if anyone hears us, I've lost all my self-preservation because of my consuming need for her. "Say the words," I demand as her back hits a wall and I dry hump her, which isn't true as I can feel her panties soaking me. When she doesn't answer, I grab her chin and give her cheeks a slight squeeze. "Open your eyes, sweetheart."

At the endearment, she does, well, as much as possible in the midst of her lust-drunk state. "Tell me what I need to hear."

I see the moment she finally accepts her fate. I know the war is far from won, but I can't this battle as a victory. Her head falls to the crook of my neck and she begins working herself against me, both of us frantically seeking what we need. Then the words I needed more than my next breath hits my ears. "I'm yours, Romeo."

"Damn right you are." And then I take her lips as I push her panties to the side and part her folds. I work her clit, my mouth leaving hers so I can hear her, and I'm rewarded when she calls my name. Her thighs quiver as she finds her release, and I can't wait to feel her do that around my dick. I might not survive it.

Chapter Seven

~ Chels ~

With his arm around my shoulder and both of us laughing, we walk out of the dressing room area, but I feel like my feet aren't touching the ground. The weight I always carry has lifted some. Romeo helps me let loose, allowing me to be myself when we're together, and I can let my guard down. Hell, he just gave me an orgasm in the middle of the boutique and I'm not ashamed about it.

"Your smile is gorgeous."

"Not so bad yourself, Ro." At that, he pulls me closer and kisses the side of my head as we head toward the door. I know this sense of security he gives me as well as the fact we just seem to fit might be temporary, but maintaining a constant shield gets tiring. I want to explore this, at least until one of us decides to move on.

"You're the only person to ever give me a nickname. I like it." His warm gaze washes over me and my thoughts begin running wild. I see a future with Romeo, the home we'd have together. I'd be able to paint and he can do…I really need to learn more about him. Even with my visual of the two of us, he's still mostly a stranger to me.

"What's on your mind?" He asks. "You're awful pensive there." I'm about to confess my attraction to him when I jump at the sound of my name. I start to pull away, but Romeo doesn't let me move, choosing instead to possessively tighten his hold, unknowingly protecting me from my grandfather. "You know this man?" I don't get a chance to answer before it's done for me.

"Of course she does. I'm her grandfather. When I heard she was here with one of the Cupids, I just had to see it for myself. I'm Leroy Smith, best damn welder in town, and I've been trying to make my way into Heartland." He extends his hand and I tense, suddenly no longer wanting to be here and wishing I could forget this whole situation. Everyone knows who he is, and I'm sure Ro does, too, and he can easily ruin my whole life. Not as if he hasn't tried before.

"I know exactly who you are. I'm just perplexed as to why you're here. As far as I'm concerned, my fiancée has no family and as long as I have a say in it, you will not step foot in my town." Dismissing my grandfather as if he's trash, this magnificent man tilts my chin and kisses me. "Sweetheart, give this credit card to the shop owner and I'll deal with this." Not sure what else to do but to follow his lead, I nod and stare in his eyes. I'm searching for some semblance of disappointment towards me, but there is none. Perhaps not everything is lost. When I return, bags in hand, they're still going at it. The old bastard's face is bright red as he spews insults aimed at me.

"She's nothing but a common whore. I've heard all the rumors. Why else would Cupid himself give this tramp half a million dollars?" Romeo is honorable to a fault, but this is not his battle. He shakes his head, silently commanding me to stay out of it, but I can't.

"I got this. He's my problem, not yours."

"Oh, but it is. I'm your man, and I won't allow him to disrespect you. Now get back to the other side until I'm done." I try to disagree, but he growls at me. I take a deep breath, forcing myself not to go off on him because he's doing this for me, but it still pisses me off.

I stomp to the counter, and the woman who has known me most of my life takes pity on me. She signals for me to follow her, so I do, letting her lead me to a small waiting area. This must be where the bride's family waits. Taking a seat, I glance around, hoping it'll distract me. Unfortunately, despite how pretty the dresses are, none truly catch my eye. I mean, not that I'll ever need one. Marriage is not something for a girl like me.

"You have a good man, and it's obvious he loves you very much. I'm glad you finally found someone that protects you." I'm speechless by her words as she hands me a tea. I had assumed the attitude when we first came in was because I'm considered trash by some.

"He's growing on me," I admit. Unable to resist as I don't understand the change in her treatment of me, I add, "This is surprising coming from you. I thought you'd want to shoot me."

"My displeasure was never at you. I hated what your parents did to you, but it wasn't my place to say anything. And honestly, you really weren't approachable whenever you'd see me." Then she pats my hand, leaning closer as if she's about to share a secret. "Also, I wasn't sure about that man of yours. I heard rumors, and believed he was taking advantage of you, which you don't deserve. Nor do you to simply be his plaything. But I realized how wrong that thought was when he stood up to your grandfather. Even if this whole thing started as a sham, he's head over heels for you now."

Footsteps approaching stop our conversation, and Ro joins us soon after, looking as dangerous as ever. There's a glint in his eyes I can't decipher, and it gives me goosebumps. He's tense, and when he helps me from the chair it's with a bit more force than needed, his voice is hard when he informs me it's time he and I had a chat.

"Really? You'll be lucky if I ever talk to you again after that stunt."

"Sweetheart, I won't apologize for protecting what's mine. Whether you've accepted that or not is on you. Now let's go, we have a flight in an hour, and I don't want to be late."

"Yeah, I don't do those. Do whatever you need to. I'll see you tomorrow." I start to back away, but I should've known better. Before I know it, I'm slung over his shoulder and his firm hand is on my ass. I don't attempt to fight or wriggle off him because it won't work in this moment. However, when we head outside to a waiting a car, I change my mind. I can only take so much embarrassment in one day, and I really don't want him to see how I'll react if he tries to get me on a plane.

Unfortunately, I underestimated his ability to read me. He slides inside without once letting go of me, then promptly sets me on his lap. "You gotta let me stay behind, otherwise, I'll be a mess the entire trip. Why is this so important? I refuse to go. Nope, not happening. In fact…" In the middle of my word vomit, he kisses me. But it's different from the others we've shared. His hands are cupping my cheeks, his lips are gentle and soft, a seemingly affectionate attempt to soothe me.

When he retreats, his gaze is directly on mine as he states, "Angel, I have a special delivery for my sister, and I want you with me because I can't handle being away from you again. I promise nothing will happen and that I will always take care of you. The universe wouldn't dare take you away from me so soon. Okay?" I agree and seeing the devotion in his eyes helps. I believe him and have a feeling he'd take on the world for me. If I'm not careful, he'll own every part of me, a fact that no longer sounds that bad. Laying my head on his shoulder, I let his warmth lull me into a state of relaxation and peace that's been missing my whole life. He moves my bangs and brushes his lips across my forehead, the gesture so intimate and sweet I never want him to stop. "You can't hide forever, Chels. Can we talk now?"

"I guess."

"Why didn't you tell me about your family? Leroy is a very well-known man; how come he treats you that way?" Taking a deep breath, I tell him everything, including why I need to leave and never return. I can feel his reactions to my story, the emotions he's experiencing throughout it, but it's my plan to leave the North Pole that affects him the most. I'd been so caught up in my own story I failed to realize he may not be able to go, nor want to for that matter. His roots are in Heartland, and unlike me, he has people that would miss him. A small part of me starts to panic because I've let him in, and the rest of the ride is eerily silent.

It feels different after that, and I'm so upset I don't even fight the plane ride, choosing instead to take a couple Benadryl as Ro suggested. My dreams once more show me what our lives could be. We're happy and in love. Everything is perfect until I come to a divide in the road, forcing me to choose whether to stay with him or follow my dreams. Something wakes me and I never make a decision…

"It's beautiful." I'm in awe as we pull up to a two-story building in the artsy downtown area. The outside is covered in graffiti that seems to depict tattoos with vines reaching upward and wrapping around the small balcony on the upper level. It looks abandoned but well taken care of. Curiosity has me leaping out of the car. A deep sigh leaves Ro as he stands beside me, and when I glance at him, sadness appears for a second before he hides it.

"This place is a masterpiece, though it has sadly been forgotten. When I'm in town, I crash here." He pauses a minute, then continues, "I don't have to be at *Carmichael Candies* until tomorrow afternoon, so let's go upstairs. I want to show you the sights and I have a special surprise for tonight. It'll give us a chance to get to know each other. I need to know all the things."

"Um…I just told you my life story, which means if anyone needs to fess up, it's you." I take notice of the engraving on the steps, the initials C.I. clearly marked on each. I want to ask what it stands for but hold back, feeling as if I don't have the right. It doesn't stop my mind from churning, and the possibility it has to do with another woman pisses me off. Needing some space, I accept the offer to use the shower. The hot water helps, leaving me almost rejuvenated.

When I return to the bedroom, I'm so shocked to see the dress I kept eyeing at the boutique that I almost drop my towel. It's an original rockabilly dress with polka dots and a gorgeous bow on the side from the nineteen fifties. Knowing how expensive it had to be, I'd drooled from afar, not even wanting to risk trying it on. Tearing my eyes from it, my gaze skates over the pair of red Mary Jane pumps and a strand of pearls I really hope aren't real. It's all so beautiful I'm almost afraid to put it on, but I'm weak and can't resist for long.

My reflection has me close to tears. The realization that he chose it for me instead of all the others shows how much he truly understands me.

And he actually listens when I talk. I'd mentioned in passing once over the phone my favorite shade of lipstick and he remembered. Feeling rather sexy, I seek him out, wanting to thank him for being so wonderful. When I don't find him, I head outside, being extra careful on the stairs as I'm not used to the heels.

I spot the entrance to the lower level slightly open and walk through it. It's pristine inside, and the walls bear the same logo I saw before as well as more graffiti. There are individual rooms, and it's then I recognize it as a tattoo shop, or what should be one.

Following the light at the end, I discover another door ajar and see Ro on a rolling chair. His elbows are on his knees, head buried in his hands. It hurts my heart to see him appear so defeated. Cautiously approaching him, I ask if he's okay, and he straightens, eyes locking on mine, gaze burning into me. I might as well not be wearing anything.

"Fuck, angel. You look like a depraved dream. Come here." I move toward him, giving a small twirl along the way. I want to be what he wants more than his next breath, and to show him he can be who he is with me. When he bites his bottom lip, I know he's holding back, and it's now my mission to break him.

Without fear of repercussions or

consequences, I decide I'm all in. I slowly lower myself to my knees, his inhale urging me on.

"Fucking Christ, what are you doing? Get up before I forget to be a gentleman with you. I almost lost it at the boutique." He tries to help me up, but I stop him with my hand on his chest. His heart is thumping so hard it feels like it's about to come out. My fingers run down his abs until I get to the edge of his pants, and I clumsily deal with the fastenings before reaching in and taking him out. Letting me know the power I have over him, he hisses in pleasure as I wrap my hand around his girth, and it turns me on more than I ever thought possible.

Chapter Eight

~ Romeo ~

I'm already leaking from the sight of her mere inches from my dick, her soft hand wrapped around it. She's such a vision in her pretty new dress, and I don't want to ruin it, but I'm only so strong.

"What's wrong, Ro? Thinking how much you want me to suck you?" Her words are pure sin, causing me to let loose with a string of fucks.

When her tongue flicks out, taking with it some of my cum, I feel the need to warn her, "Sweetheart, unless you plan on ending this torture, I suggest you stop now. I'm two seconds from pushing through your lips and using your naughty mouth as my toy." She informs me she isn't going anywhere, then tightens her grip, moving up and down ever so slowly, prolonging my agony. She aims a playful smile at me, proving I'm a puppet following her lead at this point as long as she keeps touching me.

More spurts from me and she eagerly touches it, then returns to her earlier pace. I swallow hard, chanting her name as if in prayer. Appropriate as she's my personal fucking goddess and is currently leading me to the brink of insanity.

Chels finally takes the first few inches in her mouth, continuing until I reach the back of her throat. When her tongue joins in, teasing me, I hit my limit. Taking control, I fill her mouth, holding her head as I fuck it like my life depends on it.

I look down as she moans and see her free hand under her skirt as she works her pussy, so turned on from what she's doing to me. How the hell did I get so fucking lucky? Her breathing is ragged, frustration crossing her face as she seeks relief and finds none. Pulling away, her displeasure at me doing so obvious, but if my angel needs to cum it'll be on my cock. I'm in charge of her orgasms, not her. Wasting no time, I push the now ruined thong to the side. My only regret is not getting a taste first. Perhaps I'll be calm enough after a couple rounds.

"I need you to fuck me," she begs as she arches backward.

"Shit!" Lining myself at her entrance, her pussy instantly gripping me like a vise, I push all the way in, my fingers digging into her hips. Her damn dress is so tight I can't bite her nipples as I wish, so I go for her neck instead.

"Destroy me, Ro. Own me." Her hands yank my hair, her nails score my scalp, and I welcome the pain. Using my strength, I lift her up and down my shaft, helping her match my rhythm until we're in perfect sync. Once we are, I cup her ass and squeeze it as she takes me. Knowing I'll have the memories of our first time being here of all places, has my need for her erupting ten-fold.

My movements become almost deranged with my need to claim her, to give her release she was seeking moments ago. The noises she's making in my ear have me rutting in her. Then my release hits, triggering her own as my seed fills her. I'm still as hard as when we first started, and it's all because of her. I doubt my craving for her will be satisfied until I've had her over and over, but I have something special planned, and I will not falter in showing her the town. Even if it kills me.

Once we've reluctantly separated, she freshens up in the bathroom and I turn off the lights and lock the door. I know what I have to do, the idea grabbing me with every fiber of my being, making me feel alive. And it's all because of her.

Arms around each other, we head out. It's starting to get dark, which means the town will soon be bursting with life. Our destination is the place owned by the parents of my good friends, Todd and Finley. I spent a lot of time there during college and their food is delicious. Back then it was just a small pizza joint mainly for students, but it transformed into an eclectic restaurant that hosts a different theme every night. Lucky for me, it's poetry today.

I haven't been here in at least a year, so I knew I was in for it when they saw me. As expected, there's a line already forming, one that will continually grow as the night goes on. The expression of wonder on Chels' face is priceless, further cementing what I need to do for both of us. I just need a few more days to put my plan in action.

"You'll see," I tell her when she tries to find out what we're doing. "I have a feeling you'll love it. They have the best pizza and word is this is the place to be tonight."

"Well, I'll be damned. If it isn't the fucker in the flesh! Should I kick your ass now or let my mother do it?" I hear Finley's unmistakable voice shout as she comes up closer, wearing her signature leather pants and a helmet. Todd joins us, giving his usual greeting of a nod which is the equivalent of a conversation for him as he's never been much of a talker. Despite being fraternal twins, he and Finley look a lot alike.

"Who is this gorgeous creature on your arm? It can't be your girl because you're an ugly fucker," she states, then turns to Chels. "I'm Finley, but you can call me whatever you want." She winks, and I want to kick her, but my angel doesn't miss a beat.

Chels mock whispers, "You wouldn't be able to handle me. I'm a little psycho, he just doesn't know it yet. But he can show you the marks." At this, my usually cocky friend blushes, then shakes her head at me.

"Damn, boy, no wonder you haven't been around. She's got you on a tight leash. It's a good look for you." The laugh that escapes Chels is music to my ears. She already fits in so well with me and my world. Her eyes are so full of light in this moment and I never want them to dim again. After a few minutes of shooting the shit, even Todd comes out of his shell and actually says a couple sentences.

We skip the line and head inside to a table in front, and Mrs. Anzel comes over, pizza in hand and a big smile on her face. She's always been like a mom to me and was disappointed when I decided to give up on my dream. She hugs me, then proceeds to fawn over Chelsea.

"You see this? It's what you two knuckleheads need to do, find a good woman and settle down. Don't think I didn't see that rock on her," she tells me, adding, "You got yourself a looker."

"That I do," I instantly agree.

"Does that mean you're finally coming back? Did she talk some sense into you about throwing away your dream as if it was nothing?"

"Oooooh. Mama told you," Finley taunts. "So are you?" Chels asks about my dream, not knowing the story, and they all gasp in mock horror, their unison always uncanny. Mrs. Anzel pulls up a chair and shares what I wish I could forget. I'd recently acquired my business degree and had the money I needed to open Cupid Ink when mom had called about the fake emergency. With my chance gone because of it, I'd returned to doing what I knew. Love is a pretty lucrative business, so my expenses were more than taken care of. I just had to sacrifice being myself, something I hadn't been able to do in so long.

Once a year when I'm feeling horrible after Valentine's Day while the Cupids are on vacation – we work extra hard from December to the end of January to match couples – I come here to visit my friends. It gives me the chance to enjoy their company as well as reminisce on what could've been. Unable to see the building that would've housed my dream go to ruin, too, I have someone stop in once a week to take care of it.

The soft hand squeezing mine brings me back to the present as Mrs. Anzel is finishing her tale, then she and the twins leave. Chels cups my cheek and I instinctively lean into it.

"The CI was for Cupid Ink?" I nod, unable to answer, then press a kiss to her palm. There's understanding in her eyes, and she climbs on my lap, sensing my need for a subject change. I hold her, seeking comfort, not even reacting when I probably squeeze a little tighter than normal. We stay that way for the remainder of the night, not even moving when our food arrives. She lets me feed her the pizza, and I can't help but thinking as we head home that I never want this moment to end.

Chapter Nine

~ Romeo ~

Valentine's Day...

I've tried to get my sister alone to stop her from making the biggest mistake of her life, but she's having none of it. No matter how hard I try, I can't get her to come to her senses. After picking up the candy she'd ordered, I'd spent yesterday following her around, trying to talk some sense into her. I'd even gone so far as sitting through her facial and manicure.

The Cupids are too close to breaking our tradition of matching couples by true love, and I refuse to let that happen, especially as she's the reason I met my own soulmate. Agapi deserves a love that'll last a lifetime, not one done in haste because she's lost her mind. Which means I have no choice but to be the thing I hate most…Cupid. My little sister will find love even if it means facing our mother's wrath.

With no other options, I'd called the stubborn as fuck Jack last night, only to come up empty-handed as he'd gone out of town for a month-long teaching event at a university. Which explains why he hasn't shown up. I have no doubt if he'd gotten the news about all this that he'd be here, trying to stop it, too. I'm hoping my plan C works, his sister, Sonja. She might be the only one that can reason with him. But I need to give them both time, which means enacting Operation Stall this Wedding.

Chels was fully on board with my plan after I'd explained it and will be responsible for distracting my mom while I talk to my dad. I hope to get him to agree to give Agapi and I a few minutes alone. My mom was so excited to see me with someone, a woman I'd introduced as my fiancée no less, that she's been dragging my poor angel all over.

Being the mellow guy he is, dad agrees and gets a beer from the open bar. The reception is being held beside the church in their luxury banquet hall. Knowing him, he'd much rather do this then play father of the bride yet again. Running upstairs, I find my sister sitting there, tear tracks evident on her cheeks, though she attempts to swipe them away, averting her eyes from mine.

"I've made up my mind and I'm not changing it for you or anyone else."

"If that's what you want, then okay."

Her head turns toward me so fast I'm surprised she doesn't have whiplash. "After all the crap you kept giving me, that's all you have to say now?"

"You obviously think this is the right path for you, so who am I to stand in your way? As long as you're happy, then I am, too."

"I am," she snaps, trying to sound convincing. I finally get the message I've been waiting for at that moment and start to take a step forward. I take her arm and lead her from the room. "You really are fine with this?" The perplexed look on her face is almost comical. One of the things about Agapi is you can't disagree with her. She's so stubborn she'll do the opposite just to prove a point. Hence her marrying a man she doesn't know to piss off a very stuck in his way doctor. I nod, and panic creeps into her eyes and she starts shaking.

"Good. Let's go then." If it gets to the point I need to drag her from the altar, I will, but I'll play along for now. Dad takes her arm in his as we reach our spot, and I can only hope the text was confirmation of the miracle I need to protect my sister who is currently glancing at me, reminding me of when I'd held her in my arms when she was born. The one whose knees I bandaged. My baby sister that I promised I'd always watch out for. Deep inside I know she's waiting for me to save her again, and if Lantern doesn't care enough to do it, I will.

"Stop!" Relief crosses her features and I pull her to me. Dad shrugs and moves to the side. Mom, on the other hand, seems as if she's about to murder us. She's rushing down the aisle, not a small feat for such a short woman, full of smiles and apologies to the guests.

"What in God's name are you two doing? This church is filled with our family and closest friends. Let go of your sister so she can get married."

"No!" I inform her, taking the brunt of her icy glare. "She doesn't want to. She's doing it out of rebellion, and you know it. Truly look at her, and I mean really look at her." Agapi steps out from behind me, staring at the ground, unable to face our mom, and it breaks my heart. "Has your need to be the perfect Cupid blinded you to the real reason we do this? What happened to fucking true love?"

"I... but." She's at a loss for words, though it only lasts a second. "Sometimes you have to take a chance. We gamble, it's what we do. Look at you and Chels. I know the whole thing is a sham, but you fell in love with her. Or are you going to deny your feelings?" I turn to the woman who has indeed become the center of my world, and if I hadn't taken the chance...

The next words out of my mouth will either solidify us or make her run from me. If she chooses the latter, I'll never stop chasing her. Looking my angel straight in the eyes, I admit, "Yes, I love her.

Obsessively, deliriously, and completely." Her gasp echoes in the otherwise silent room, and I want to run to her, to assure her I mean them, beg her not to be afraid, but duty keeps me from doing any of it.

Footsteps can be heard a moment before the church doors bursts open. "Agapi, stop!" Dr. Lantern almost falls over in his attempt to not crash into my mom as he frantically searches for my sister. When he sees her, he yanks her to him and says, "Fuck, I thought I lost you. Are you insane? I said to live, not give me a heart attack! You didn't even give me a choice in this!"

"But you s-said…" She stutters, obviously not understanding what's happening.

"That you're too young and need to follow your dreams, not marry the first man you saw."

"Being a wife to you and a mom to your kids are my dreams, however, you disregarded me and my wants. And now you think you can just march in here and I'll accept it?"

"Yes." The smack she gives him, letting him know that was not the right answer, causes everyone to snicker. But it only causes him to hold her tighter.

"Let go of me. You're interrupting my wedding. I still plan on getting married."

"Yeah Buttercup, to me," he demands. "I can guarantee I'll never let you go again, and I promise to knock you up with a couple babies to keep you good and content."

"All right, that's it. I'm out," I state. "What is it with you guys always talking about my sisters and what you want to do with them? Fucking Luca and Stefano each time I see them, and now you, too?" I head toward my Chels, figuring everything will be okay.

"Does this mean the wedding is off? If so, I'm going to the game." The groom appears unconcerned at the turn of events. His parents are shaking their heads at his attitude, but he ignores them and throws a peace sign at my sister before leaving.

Where the hell did my mom find this idiot?

Chapter Ten

~ Chels ~

So much happened at once I'm not sure if I can process it all. Truth is, while everything was pretty unbelievable, his words reminded me to breathe. He confessed in a room full of people that he loves me, and the truth of it was in his eyes. Now I just have to figure out what to do with the knowledge. Romeo is a definite wrench in my plans.

"Hey." All I can manage is to repeat it when he stands next to me and takes my hand in his before placing a kiss on it. "We'll talk when we get out of here, okay?" He asks, and I nod, not knowing what else to do. Half the guests start exiting the church, clearly those from the groom's side. I can't imagine what Agapi is feeling, though she truly doesn't seem to care from what I can see. She's in the arms of the guy she loves, and he appears to feel the same about her.

Looking at my own man, the one who makes me feel things I never have before, I know I'd choose him time and time again. I may not ever make it to the place I've always wanted to go but losing my chance at true love would be my biggest regret. Decision made, I squeeze his hand in reassurance and some of his vulnerability fades. Meanwhile, his mom is standing there visibly embarrassed and unable to speak. We haven't really interacted that much, but she's taken a liking to me. I know she adores them and would never intentionally hurt any of them.

"Well," she begins, "there's no point in crying over spilled milk. You two head to the front. Lovin Cupid is getting a wedding out of this, and since you ruined my plans, your ass better be ready to marry my daughter," she informs Jack, then she hands her daughter to Mr. Cupid and marches the newcomer to the end of the aisle. Agapi protests, saying this is not the way, but her steps are a lot faster than those of the usual wedding march. The ceremony starts and my eyes get misty as they say their vows, speaking from their hearts instead of using the traditional ones. I'm wiping away a tear as they kiss when Romeo tugs on my arm.

When he says we should go, I tell him we can't yet. "Your whole family expects us at the reception. It wouldn't be right to not show," I whisper, trying not to draw attention to us. He gives me a look that tells me I need to do as he says, and I swear I melt and get mad at the same time. He knows how much it pisses me off when he does that, but the fact that he still does sends liquid heat traveling straight to my nipples and down to my pussy.

"I'm not asking. There's nothing here for us, and we have somewhere else to be." Testing him, I shake my head and he immediately stands, throwing me over his shoulder, and setting his hand on my ass to keep my dress from flying up.

"I can walk."

"Obviously, you can't listen, though." His voice is rougher than normal, his muscles tense, letting me know something is wrong. And I want to know what it is right now. But people are watching us, and my cheeks are on fire from embarrassment. His mom is shouting for us, but Romeo's long strides carry us through the door in seconds as he ignores her.

"Ro, please let me down. I promise I'll go with you," I attempt to reason with him, using a soothing voice, and some of his intensity dissipates. At the car, he sets me down, my body sliding down his before he traps me against the passenger door. His eyes have a dark edge to them, and I place my hand on his cheek. He leans into it, then places his on top of it, as if afraid I'll move mine. "You going to tell me what's wrong?"

He pleads, "First, promise that you are in this with me?"

I take a deep breath, telling him, "I am, and I'm not going anywhere." Then I pause because the words I'm about to say are completely foreign to me, but no less true. "I love you, Romeo."

He exhales like he'd been holding his breath in anticipation. "About fucking time you realize it. I've been in love with you since the first time you looked up from the booth."

"Is that so? Was this your whole plan? Charm me until I couldn't stay away? I never stood a chance, did I?" He shakes his head, then rests his forehead on mine.

"Once my sister said I do, it dawned on me that you'd be done. Our contract was over, and that fact was driving me crazy. I couldn't risk you leaving without giving me a fighting chance. Marry me?" He blurts, continuing without letting me answer. "Before you say no, I'm not going to stop asking. I'll do so every hour for the rest of our lives until you do. And you already have the ring. I'm not letting you take it off." His words feed the emptiness that had been part of me for so long.

This bossy, aggravating man won me over in days, erasing so much pain from my life. In his eyes, I'm perfect, and he doesn't just say so, but he shows me, too. The way his hold tightens when we're in public, his need to kiss me even when we both knew it wasn't due to this arrangement. He only has my best interests at heart.

"If you insist on stalking me until I say yes, I guess I better do as you want."

Appearing amused at my response, he smiles. "Look at that, my Chels is finally coming around to my way of thinking. Next thing I know I'll have a docile little wife." I go to knee him in the balls, but he dodges me before I connect, but the big goof still feigns being hurt.

I take the opportunity to pull his keys out of his pocket and warn him, "Now I'm gonna drive your Porsche. Since we're all in, let's go pick up our daughter from Molly."

"Our what?" I repeat myself, adding her name, Kat, and he blinks, as if that will help him understand what I'm telling him. Ducking to escape, I walk to the driver's seat, giggling as he asks, "You mean you have a cat, right?" Then he places his hand on his chest and sighs with relief, like he'd almost had a heart attack. "Whew, you gave me a scare."

"I have a dog named Kat. She's a sweetheart and will eventually get used to you. Fair warning, she doesn't like men and will bite you." Laughing, I have to tease him by adding, "You should've seen your face, though. Would me having a kid have been a deal-breaker?"

"Nothing would be with you, but I'd like to think a child would've been mentioned before this. Plus, I would have had the urge to end the man you would always be attached to."

"Is that so?"

"Shit, you could be pregnant now. I hadn't been with anyone in so long I didn't think to use protection," he confesses.

"Calm down, lover boy, I have an IUD. Kids were never part of my plan."

"Good, I'm a selfish bastard when it comes to you and don't want to share you with anyone. Now let's go to your place, mine will be filled with people. Tomorrow will be a long day for us, and I want you to myself tonight." Surprised, I ask what we're doing, but he doesn't explain, just gets comfortable as if he's on top of the world.

After being loved numerous times during the night, I wake up, disappointed I'm not wrapped in the arms of the man I'll never get enough of. The smell of breakfast fills the air and I drag myself from the bed, my stomach already growling. I hardly ate yesterday, and I know I burned more calories than I usually do in a week trying to keep up with Romeo's insatiable need for me. My first mission is to get coffee, the holy elixir that will bring me back to life.

On the way to the kitchen, I begin to notice my things are missing, sealed boxes here and there and start to freak out a bit. I know I agreed to all this, but I didn't think he meant right away. A small gasp leaves my lips as some of them are picked up by men I don't recognize and taken outside, and that's when he sees me.

His eyes go dark as he sees what I'm wearing, or the lack of. "Get in that fucking room and put on some clothes unless you want me in jail before I even get to feed you." He's staring at me like I'm about to get it, fueling a naughty vixen inside me that only he brings forth. Instead of doing as he says, I shake my head no and bite my lip. The poor mover that was about to walk between us keeps his gaze focused on the floor, frozen in place.

"I'd prefer caffeine and your explanation on why I should change when this is what I wear every morning? Not my fault you decided to do this without informing me." Stepping forward until I'm in front of him, the stranger sees his chance and runs out the door so fast he almost trips. Looking at Romeo's boxers, seeing that he's hard for me again,

I want to push him. How far can I go before he snaps? My answer comes a moment later when a couple more guys come in just as I'm rubbing his cock over the material.

"Everybody get the fuck out. Now!

"But sir, the truck isn't filled yet, and we have…"

"Leave or it'll go up in flames," he declares in such a vicious tone it sends shivers down my spine. Knowing he's contemplating a felony just to stop them from seeing me has my pussy drenched. "Don't fucking move," he growls, then stomps toward the door to lock it. Taking advantage of the fact he can't see what I'm doing, I strip off my short nightie, leaving only my lace panties on, and lay on the kitchen table.

When he turns, finding me spread out in offering, he appears to be in actual physical pain from trying to hold back. He'd made slow love to me last night, but I want hard and fast now. "Baby, you're killing me. I can't promise to be easy on you. I'm too on edge from those men seeing the body that is only meant for me. We need to get going and moved to our apartment."

"What are you talking about? And where's Kat? I ask."

"On her way to Mrs. Anzel. She's babysitting until I get us settled in." Sitting upright, I try to decipher his words. "Don't look so shocked, angel. I told you I'd make all your dreams come true. I'm leaving it all behind and starting over with you, a brand-new life where you can go as you please and never have to think of this place again."

"Are you for real? What about your family? Oh, your mom will hate me! Won't you get disowned if you're no longer a Cupid?"

"You're all that matters. Besides, I've made investments, so I don't need to be a Cupid to take care of you. I just want to be your husband. Now lay back down. I've changed my mind. We have time for me to lick that sweet cream between your legs."

"You're going to end up in hell if you don't change your ways, Mr. Dirty," I warn him.

"I'll gladly burn as long as I can fuck you senseless, lick you dry, and own that ass for the rest of my days," he informs me with no regret.

"Fuck, I think we'll both burn then."

Epilogue

~ Romeo ~

Five years later…

My heart swells with pride as I pull up to Cupid Ink because I finally have the life I always wanted. When we opened the doors four years ago, I was the happiest I've ever been. It took meeting Chels to open my eyes to everything I was missing, and neither of us looked back after leaving our respective homelands, nor have we dwelled on our pasts there. We caused quite the stir, causing some rules to be changed, and I'd like to think we made a difference for the generations to come.

Cupids now have the choice to stay in the family business or venture out. Of course, if you choose the latter, you have to make it on your own with minimal help from your parents, but that's true of every kid as they grow up. Kent and John Alexander call regularly to chat, as does my family. Such as the recent conversation with my aunt letting us know Chels' grandfather had passed, and while she doesn't wish ill on anyone, not even him for how he treated her, she doesn't owe them shit.

We've created not one, but two very successful businesses – the premier tattoo shop in the state, and her studio, Stupid Cupid Designs, affectionately named after her favorite man and attached to my shop. I love storming in there and throwing her over my shoulder. Her employees have long since accepted this as normal behavior for us, so it doesn't even faze them now. It makes her mad as hell, though I know she mostly feigns outrage on my behalf because she loves it when I go all caveman on her.

Today, I've been warned to be on my best behavior, something I seem to have a problem with, as yet another comic book publisher will be visiting with an offer. He's wasting his time as we've already decided to go with a small local indie company, but my wife didn't want to be rude. We'll meet, listen to what they have to say, then decline later via letter. Apart from the artwork she creates on her easels, she also started a comic book about the adventures of a relentless Cupid which is loosely based on my mother. She's actually in town and equally as excited as Chels.

Thankfully, her meddling is now only fiction. Considering how things played out, I'm glad that they get along so well. The fact that Chels views her as the mom she never had just makes it all the sweeter.

That's not to say there weren't obstacles in our path. Mom did disown me for six months but came around when all of her children returned the favor. Dad, one of the most influential Cupids, defied her for the very first time when he spoke to the council on our behalf and getting them to agree to letting us leave in peace. But the final blow was when the twins turned their backs on her, informing her if some of us were no longer family then none of us were.

Opening the door, I wonder if the meeting was cancelled after all when I don't see Chels or my mom. Not that I'd mind as I hate when they attempt to get extra friendly with my wife. She can sit there and say I'm wrong, but I know those fuckers want a piece of her, and it's only my mom reminding them she's married to her son that saves their lives, often repeating it so many times I have to laugh. Okay, so my mom isn't completely done meddling, but at least she's using her powers for good in this case. She's more worried about losing her favorite daughter-in-law than saving my ass.

"Where's my angel?" I ask one of her assistants, an unmotivated intern. Her name is Jess, Jaz, or something like that. I've told my wife to find another as there's plenty lining up to work for her, but she has a soft heart and refuses to do so. I don't push it because I want her to be happy, but if she worked for me, I'd have fired her ass months ago.

True to form, she barely glances at me, just shrugs, and goes back to her phone. "With some dude in the writing studio."

Fire ignites in my veins. "My mother, too?" I want to know, hoping she says yes before I really lose my shit. Her response of nope is the last straw. All the interns are paid, thanks to me, and to continue receiving that salary my only rule is that they never leave my wife alone when there's a man present. They are my eyes and ears around here.

"Get the fuck out! You're fired!" I yell, her only reaction another shrug as she grabs her bag and proceeds to stroll toward the door. I rush towards the back room, and sure enough, there's a guy standing shoulder to shoulder with her, the two of them laughing as if they're lifelong friends. I stalk closer and pull her behind me, fighting the urge to strangle him as I inform him, "We don't want your business. Leave!"

"Babe," she chimes in as she touches my arm, but nothing can stop me now.

"No! He's taken advantage of your politeness and sweetness. I will not have him looking at your body. I pay your interns to make sure no one is near you without someone else present." As soon as the words are out of my mouth, I know I'm in big fucking trouble. She knows how growly I can get, but not the lengths my obsession goes to.

He laughs hysterically, adding to my annoyance, stating, "When you told me your husband was crazy, I almost didn't believe it. Girl, he's a snack, I can see why you guard him as well." He extends his hand, but I scoff at it. I don't give a shit that he's gay, he's still a man that was left alone with my wife.

"Romeo Cupid Junior, I swear to all that is holy you are getting worse by the day. This is Michael, my new permanent assistant. He'll be keeping an eye on the place." She steps between us, poking me with her finger. "You were the one that said I need someone to help me. You want me to cut back on hours so we can spend more time together, right?" She raises her voice accusingly, leaving me a bit speechless as that's exactly what I mentioned three days ago. Of course, I meant a woman, yet another thing I mistakenly say out loud.

The fire that burns in her eyes at that has me fearing for my life and making my dick hard. I want to take her to my soundproof office and fuck her until she forgets everything else. "I know that look and it isn't happening, Ro. You're in the dog house, so don't even try it."

"Like hell I am. Michael, you're hired, and you're closing today," I say, then throw him my spare key for the place, and lift my wife, her kicking and screaming as I carry her to the front. The customers next door at my shop are not our regulars and their eyes widen, but my artists laugh. I enter my office, remembering to lock the door, and place her on my desk.

Settling between her open legs I grip her hips and declare, "What is this about me being in trouble, my little hellcat? Katrine doesn't even have a dog house. Her, Rufus, and Lester sleep with us," I remind her of just how needy our children are. Yes, they're the four-legged kind, but that's exactly what we wanted.

"Don't act cute. You know damn well your jealousy is stupid," she says, lying through her teeth. Her eyes are glazed, and her nipples are evident under the fabric of her cotton dress.

"Not acting cute, sweetheart. I don't share. What's mine is only mine to love, spoil, kiss, touch, and definitely fuck." A shiver leaves her at my words. Her eyes are half-closed, her labored breath, almost begging for it. I lean forward, slowly sliding my hands up her torso and running my thumbs over her pebbled tips. "You did that shit on purpose. You knew he'd drive me over the fucking edge. You wanted me to bring you in here, turn you over, and fuck that sweet pussy of yours until you were screaming so loud the soundproofed doors wouldn't even stop them from hearing you. Isn't that right?" I whisper before placing a kiss behind her ear.

"Fuck."

"I'll take that as a yes. Clothes gone, baby. I need to get in the tight snatch of yours before I fucking become deranged." She moans, and always the rebel, stands and pulls her dress off, showing me that she's been running around without panties or bra, and I fucking love the devilish grin that curves her lips. Instead of doing as I ask, she returns to the desk and props herself up on her elbows, spreading herself like a feast.

"You wanna be all fuck this, fuck that, and bang on your chest outside these doors, you have to pay up. On your knees," she demands, as if that shit is a punishment. I get in position, and roughly place her legs over my shoulders, then give her a lick. The moment her juiciness hits my tongue it's fucking game over and I lap at her like a starving man. She's soon shaking uncontrollably, and I love knowing her cream will coat my desk by the time we're done. My depraved ass will rub it in as if it was wood polish, eager to enjoy a cup of coffee here with the smell of what I fucking do to her surrounding me.

"Romeo, that feels so good. Get up here and fuck me. I need you inside me." She screams when I insert two fingers inside her while sucking her clit, her body thrashing with pleasure.

"Patience, angel. I want to endure every last bit of punishment I deserve," I growl against her center before diving back in with more vigor than before. I'm not quitting until she's cum on my tongue at least twice.

It isn't until hours later that we emerge looking every bit as disheveled as we should, but there's no walk of shame. We love showing the whole damn world how fucking crazy we are for each other. I slap her ass and my girl doesn't disappoint, instead digging her nails into my own. The artists all start their hollers and catcalls, and I can't fucking wait to get her upstairs for a repeat. Our babies are just gonna have to wait outside the bedroom until we are finished. A few dog treats will convince them to forgive us.

Mistletoe
Holiday Hearts Series
PIXIE CHICA

Treat You
Better
A Stepbrother Romance
PIXIE CHICA

About the Author

Most days you can find Pixie running around trying to juggle 100 hats…one of which is Author. BTW, she still can't believe that's what she gets to call herself that. What started out as a passion for book blogging turned into publishing her very first novella… *Sealed With A Kiss.*

Pixie who is part of the LGBT Community, writes MF, FF and MM stories that are sexy, insta-love stories full of heart and with a HEA.

Her characters not only fall quickly, deeply, but are also possessive in nature. If she's not writing, then she's on Facebook…Tell her to get the hell out of there and get writing.

"Where Love Always Wins."

You can follow Pixie Chica via any of the social media by clicking the link below:
https://linktr.ee/pixiechica

Books by Pixie

Always & Forever Series
Sealed with a Kiss
In Plain Sight

Love Unexpected Series
Love at Sunset
Undeniable Love
Unleashed Love

Valladares Family Saga
Ivy's Rebellion

Tattooed Brides Series
Loved by Her
Loved in the Dark

Lancaster Falls Series
Because of Blue
Because of You

Holiday Hearts
Mistletoe
Undercover Santa
His Christmas Delivery
Stupid Cupid
Altared

Sweetville
Put a Ring on It
Stranded Christmas
Ring of Fire
Good Cop Bad Girl
Happenstance

Latimer Ladies
New Year's Kiss
Sweetness
Last Shot

Price Industries
Mine by Christmas
Give into Temptation

Sizzle Beach
Things We Did Last Summer

Standalones
A Wolfe's Ruby
A Royal Payne
Treat You Better
Teacher's Pet
Playing for Keeps
Curves Rx
My Vampire Mate

Box Sets
Holiday Hearts Collection
The Covingtons
Price Industries